Dick and Jane

READING COLLECTION • VOLUME 3

W9-CFK-768

Jump and Run

GROSSET & DUNLAP • NEW YORK

Puff

Jump, Puff.

Jump, jump, jump.

Jump, Puff, jump.

Run, Puff.

Run, Puff, run.

Run, run, run.

Jump, jump, jump.

Oh, Puff.

Oh, oh, oh.

Funny, funny Puff.

Spot

Come, come.

Come, Spot, come.

Run, run, run.

Jump, Spot.

Jump, jump.

Jump, Spot, jump.

Jump, Spot.

Jump, jump.

Jump, Spot, jump.

Jump and Play

Sally said, "Oh, look.
Mother can jump.
Mother can jump and play."

Dick said, "Jump, Father.
You can jump.
You can jump and play."

"Look, Mother," said Sally.

"See Father jump.

See Father jump and play.

Big, big Father is funny."

Jane said, "Oh, Father.
You can not jump and play.
Spot can not jump and play."

Dick said, "Oh, see Puff.
Puff can jump.
Puff can jump and play."

Run and Help

Run, Jane.

Help Mother.

Run, Jane, run.

Help Mother work.

Come, Sally, come.

Come and help.

Come and help Mother.

Run, run, run.

Look, Sally, look.

See Spot work.

Funny, funny Spot.

Oh, oh, oh.

Spot can help Mother.

See Puff Jump

Look, Dick.

See Puff jump.

Oh, look.

Look and see.

See Puff jump and play.

Come, Jane, come.

Come and see Puff.

See Puff jump and run.

See funny little Puff.

Oh, oh, oh.

See little Puff run.

Oh, see Puff.

Funny little Puff.

Spot and Tim and Puff

Spot can jump.

Little Puff can jump.

Look, Tim, look.

See Spot and Puff play.

Look, Tim.

See Sally jump.

See Sally jump down.

Down, down, down.

Sally can jump and play.

Oh, Puff.

See funny little Tim.

See Tim jump down.

Down, down, down.

Tim can jump and play.

Oh, See

Look, Sally, look.

Look down.

Look down, Sally.

Look down, down, down.

Look up, Sally.

Look up, up, up.

Run, Sally, run.

Run and jump.

Run and jump up.